The Big Blue Hen

written & illustrated by

Trish O'Leary

designed by Carla Sternberg Koch

farmer Treat

Once upon a hill lived a big blue hen named Brooder in a little Orange, Connecticut barnyard. She was no longer a great layer, but could she brood!

She brooded over cholesterol and the fact that people no longer called her eggs "nature's perfect food." She brooded over the artificial eggs that had weaseled their way into supermarket dairy cases. She brooded over statistics on how the Kentucky Fried Chickens consumed in just one year could circle the earth 13 times. And she brooded over Frank Perdue's endless palaver about "perfect bodies" and "plump chicken parts."

But most of all, she brooded over fate and the future. She was, she knew,

7

the mixer

one of the last "free-range" chickens. Already, thousands of chicks like her were toiling away their entire lives in the poultry processing industry. In places with no fresh air. No sunshine. Artificial lights.

Places where thousands just milled around under the corrugated tin roofs until the day "their time came."

Over and over, Brooder's farmer friend would patiently explain that poultry processing was just one more example of what he called "consolidation" and "technological progress," and "efficiencies made possible by economies of scale." But Brooder would hear none of it. She'd just flutter her big blue feathers

barnyard promenade

and balk in indignant reply ("balk... balk...balk") and brood on.

What a far crow from the glory days of Wild Jungle Fowl, history's first recorded chicken, Brooder felt.

It thrilled Brooder to say that very name aloud, "Wild Red." Nodding off in her own nest late at night, in her mind's eye she sometimes pictured Wild Red proudly stalking the great forests of Southeast Asia aeons ago, alongside the lumbering elephants and sleek snowy leopards and all manner of majestic creatures.

"What a comedown to live in this day and age," Brooder clucked. "Chicks strut around here as if they're something special just because someone makes a fuss over

no poultry processing

distraught & distressed

their bright red wattles and combs! And what do these pretty young pullets spend all their time doing? Preen, preen, preen. If they end up nothing but feathers and fat by the age of 18 months, it serves them right. These show-offs just make humans think that chickens are nothing but vain and silly creatures."

Brooder was not against grooming, of course. She liked her daily dirt baths. She kept her own nest tidy, pecked away at parasites...but her looks weren't what they once had been. Her comb had become cool to the touch and taken on a bluish tint. Her leg scales were horny and had lost their lustre. Her feet and claws had hardened.

Truth to tell, Brooder was no spring chicken. She was far far past 18 months.

"Who cares if my egg-laying days are over?" she'd snap. "Hens today don't even get to spend 21 days with a laid clutch anyway. Snatched away as fast as they're laid, right out from under them."

With each passing day, Brooder became a bit more peevish. She sensed her time was coming, yet she felt unfulfilled.

She'd always known she'd never be a barnyard favorite. Never hold a nest in the Great Chicken Hall of Fame. Why couldn't she let go of idle wishes and accept her feathered fate?

Yet she longed to somehow leave her scratch in history, even if that scratch merely marked one chicken's last stand...

big blue hen on grassy hill

reading the change

the hen venturer

The very next day, Brooder was gone from the barnyard. Word got around: "Brooder's a Barnyard Dropout!" The *Poultry Tribune* said it all: "Chicken Suffers Career Crisis." The photo showed her as she pickity-pecked her way out the barnyard gate, towards the road.

the chicken crosses the road

But when she got to the roadside, Brooder stopped. Look at that traffic! How could she possibly get past those whizzing cars and trucks? She was no fool...in touch with her own body enough to know that her wings weren't just short, they lacked muscle power besides. Damned evolution!

What could she do? Make a run for it? Would exercise help? A quick change in diet? More will power? Do they have motivational tapes for chickens?

Overwhelmed by so many possibilities, Brooder plopped down in the grass by the road and brooded once more...

Just then, a friendly vegetarian walking up the hill looked over and sensed the plight of this big blue hen. She helped

case library

eavesdropping

Brooder across the road in safety – no questions asked.

And on the other side of the road, down the hill, stood the town library. Its back door was open.

While Brooder was a romantic, she had a practical streak as well, and was eager to find shelter and drink before night fall. So in the door she went.

Deep in the library storage area, Brooder made herself a nest. She got the water and food she needed by periodic forays to the horse barn next to the library.

To stave off loneliness, every Tuesday and Saturday morning, Brooder pickity-pecked her way to the ventilator shaft, where she could hear the library story lady two floors above.

she saw a farm

story lady two floors above.

Inspired by the story lady's words, Brooder taught herself to read. She started with picture books and worked her way through the children's section and into the general library. At night, she supplemented her studies by playing *Sesame Street* videos on the library VCR.

The more Brooder read, the more she became aware that Wild Red Jungle Fowl had not been the world's only great chicken. She learned of the Little Red Hen, that fine-feathered female entrepreneur who was the first of her kind to earn an independent living. A bit envious of Little Red Hen's tiny chicken feet (Brooder herself was a size 10) and her stylish print aprons, Brooder

she saw a barn

she saw a library

was filled with admiration when she realized the Little Red Hen owned her very own home and displayed feminine fortitude even when frightened by a fox.

One Sunday afternoon, browsing the stacks at her leisure, Brooder came upon Chaucer's *Canterbury Tales* in the 821c section. She paused when she saw a picture of a handsome rooster and his consort labeled "Chanticleer and Dame Pertelote." For the next seven days, Brooder pretended that she too was a Chaucerian chicken who could dream great dreams and cluck in melodious Middle English.

The following Sunday, looking for travel books, Brooder found herself scanning the index of a book on a shelf

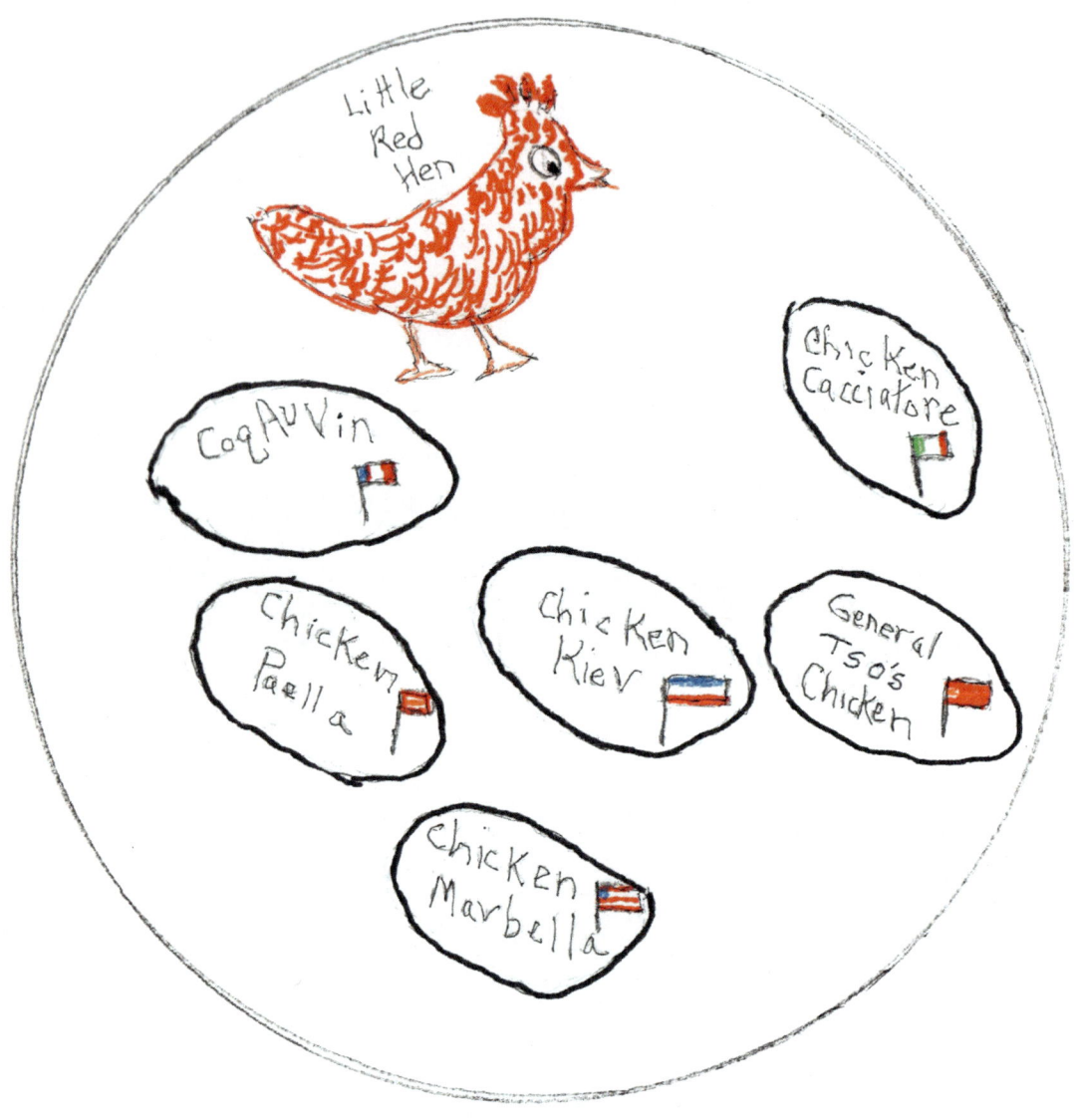

Brooder's heroes

marked 641. Her eyes got bigger and bigger...Chicken Cacciatore? Chicken Kiev? Coco Vin? General Tso's Chicken? Who were these world travelers, these foreign exotics? Why had she never heard of them before?

Brooder's reading fanned her passion for recognition. Within a week of studying a book called *Dream Jobs,* on the 331.7 shelf, Brooder pecked out her resume, one letter at a time, on the battered typewriter behind the library front desk.

Within a month, her interview at a local radio station led to a demo tape for "Chick Chat, the DIAL 1-800-CHICKEN call-in show." And her news release to the town paper, "How to hold an authentic hen party," generated enthusiastic responses. Brooder was winging it.

In the final months of her life, Brooder was offered a way to outlive fate. The broadcast engineer from her radio call-in show taped her medley of feathered folk songs for re-broadcast in hen houses throughout the country. These songs – including "Ah, Poor Bird, " "The Hen of Constant Sorrow," "I Had a Rooster" and a special rendition of "Home on the Range" – became classic favorites in chicken coops everywhere. Brooder, in the meantime, passed peacefully on to her final nesting place.

A year later, a memorial was unveiled at the town library. Known as the Great Wishing Wing, it was often visited by those eager to find comfort and help in the right places.

hen party

Made in the USA
Middletown, DE
03 April 2020